The Adventures of Naughty Nico

FINDING HIDDEN TREASURE

Best Selling Author of Children's Books

P. D. Adler

© 2013 SunVision Media
All Rights Reserved

Finding Hidden Treasure

"The Adventures of Naughty Nico"
Volume #1
First Edition

Copyright © 2013 by P. D. Adler

Published by SunVision Media
Printed in the United States of America

ISBN-13: 978-1495200465

ISBN-10: 1495200469

Learn more information or contact the author at:
http://sunvisionmedia.blogspot.com

AVAILABLE ON KINDLE DEVICES

Presented to:

From:

Date:

DEDICATION

I dedicate this book to all of my students at the Mannington Middle School where I spent time teaching as a Substitute Teacher.

"The Eagle Street Gang"

Nico. "Leader of the Gang"

It seems that wherever I go I get into trouble. Mom says I'm very active and I'm always on the go. We live on Eagle Street and I am the leader of the "Eagle Street Gang." There are four of us in the gang and we do everything together.

Ozzie

Ozzie is my best friend and loves pizza. He can eat a whole pizza by himself. He likes to have fun and getting into trouble as much as I do. I saw him eat a bug once.

Nathan

Nathan can do anything! His mom says he can find trouble before trouble finds him. He likes to play baseball and his favorite food is ice cream.

Cody

Cody is kind of shy and doesn't talk much. He doesn't mind getting his hands and clothes dirty and his favorite food is chicken nuggets.

"Finding Hidden Treasure"

An auction house is a place where people go to buy and sell things and the person willing to pay the most for something gets to buy the item.

It was a Saturday morning and Nico and his gang of 8 year boys called "The Eagle Street Gang" were bored so Nico decided that they should check out the auction house...

"Hey, what's going on in there?" asked Nathan.

"It's an auction," said Nico, "You can buy lots of stuff that other people don't want."

"I want a PIZZA," said Ozzie.

"Let's go watch," said Cody.

"Follow me boys, I'll bet we'll
have a lot of fun in here,"
Nico told the gang.

The man running the auction
was trying to sell a vase.
"Who will give me $50 for this
beautiful vase?"

"NATHAN, DON'T STICK
YOUR FINGER IN THE VASE!"
Ozzie yelled.

"I'LL GIVE YOU $50!"
yelled a man across the room.

"OH NO, I think my finger
is stuck."

The auctioneer man yelled, "GONE, SOLD FOR $50!"

"STOP!!" yelled the man who bought the vase.

"Nico, Please help me get this thing off my finger, it's stuck."

"NO!, Your going to break it!" said the man.

"But it's stuck Mister, how am I going to get it off?"

"You're coming with me," said the man, "I'll find a way to get that off your finger."

Being the leader of the gang, Nico spoke up and said, "Where he goes we all go! Me and the gang stick together like glue."

"OK, then let's go. I haven't got all day. And please be careful and don't break my expensive vase."

"I'll be careful," said Nathan.

"Hey Mister, I'm hungry, do you have any PIZZA?" asked Ozzie.

"Follow me boys, right this way...."

"Boy Mister, this is a BIG house, I'll bet I can find plenty of things to do in here," said Nico.

"Look at all of these neat things," said Nathan.

The man asked, "Will you please not touch anything boys."

Ozzie looked up at the BIG stairway and said, "I'll bet that would make a fun slide."

"You guys wait here, I'll call
the doctor to see how to get
the vase off your finger."

"DOCTOR! I don't want to see
a doctor, I'm not sick," cried
Nathan.

Nico had an idea and said to
Nathan, "don't worry about it,
I've got a great idea."

Nico runs up the stairs with the gang following and says, "Come on guys, this is going to be great. Let's get the vase off Nathan's finger before the Doctor comes."

"Come on Nathan, you're going to take a steam bath."

"Gee Nico, I just took a bath yesterday," complained Nathan.

"The steam will shrink your finger and the vase will slide right off," Nico told Nathan.

"WOW! This water is hotter than a PIZZA right out of the oven," complained Nathan.
"Did someone say PIZZA?" asked Ozzie.

"WOW! It's foggy in here, are we in a cloud?" asked Cody.

"No Cody, it's steam and I better turn off this hot water before we ALL shrink and our pants fall off," replied Nico.

"Now for a little oil around your finger and the vase should just slide right off," said Nico.

"Boy that's a lot of oil! WATCH OUT NICO, you're getting oil all over the floor," complained Nathan.

"Line up guys, it's time for a
tug a war. Let's get this vase
off of Nathan's finger," Nico
told the gang.

"EVERYBODY NOW -
PULL!"

"OH NO!!" cried the man,

"Please STOP! You'll break the vase. The doctor is on his way. PLEASE STOP!"

"HURRAY!" yelled Nathan,
"I'm FREE! Thanks guys."

"I'm slipping on all the oil,
LOOK OUT BELOW," yelled Nico.

"SOMEONE CATCH MY VASE,"
screamed the man.

"I'LL CATCH IT MISTER, I play
catch all the time with my Dad,"
Ozzie yelled.

"Oh NO! It's stuck on MY finger now!" cried Ozzie, "Oh well, at least I caught it and it didn't break."

"Now what do we do?"
Cody asked Nico.
"I don't know, it'll take forever
to shrink Ozzie's finger,"
said Nico.

"Okay mister, you win, let's go
downstairs and wait for the
doctor," Ozzie told the man.

"OH BOY!
This is going to be fun. Follow
me guys, we've got to try
sliding down the railing," yelled
Ozzie as he ran towards the
stairs.

"PLEASE BE CAREFUL, YOU'LL BREAK MY VASE!!" called the man as he ran down the stairs.

"WEEE, THIS IS FUN!"
yelled Ozzie.

"I'm right behind you,"
yelled Nico.

"OH NO! That sounded like my
vase breaking into tiny pieces.
I can't look," cried the man.

"You BROKE my vase!" said the man running down the stairs.

" Don't worry mister, we can put it back together, we're good at puzzles," said Ozzie.

"That was Fun," laughed Cody, "Thanks for breaking my fall, Ozzie."

"HEY LOOK!" said Ozzie,
"There's a 'GOLD' coin in
the vase."

"HOLY COW!"

It WAS a gold coin worth a lot of money.

"If it would not have been for you boys, I would not have found this coin. Thank you boys," said the man.

"This is a RARE coin worth a lot of money," the excited man said.

"The gang and I are good at finding things like that. You're lucky we FOUND YOU," Nico told the man.

"Come on boys, you deserve a treat. Let's go get some ice cream," the man said.

"I want Chocolate," said Nathan. "Me too," said Cody. "I want a strawberry shake," said Nico. "Do they have PIZZA?" asked Ozzie.

"Give them ANYTHING they want, I'll pay for everything," the man said to the clerk at the ice cream shop.

"Are you sure? It looks like they can eat a LOT," the clerk said back to the man.

"Boy I'm FULL," said Ozzie,
"But I'll be hungry again soon.
"I'm so full, I can hardly walk,"
said Nathan.

"I couldn't eat another bite,"
said Nico.
"But who will pay for it the
next time?" asked Cody.

"COME ON GUYS, I've got a
great idea on how we can get
more ice cream anytime we want
it," said Nico with a smile.

As the gang walked back to the
auction house, Nico explained
his plan.

"Hey MISTER!" yelled Nico,
"We're back, and my hand
is stuck!!"

In Fact...

They were ALL Stuck!!

THE END!

Thank you for buying and reading this book. I hope you have enjoyed reading it as much as I have enjoyed writing it for you.

To find my other books, including more from the Naughty Nico Series, and to get:

A "FREE" NAUGHTY NICO EBOOK

PLEASE VISIT MY WEBSITE:

http://sunvisionmedia.blogspot.com

Visit my Amazon Author Site for new releases:

http://www.amazon.com/P.-D.-Adler/e/B00EAM4VIG

I also enjoy interacting with my customers and if you have any comments or would like to contact me, please use my email address, padler@gmail.com. I try to personally answer every email within 24 hours.

Sincerely,

P. D. Adler